TALE OF THE REBEL

AMBER HARRIS

Prologue

Living in the United Stated is supposed to be a perfect existence, it is 2026, and life is hell. 2015 is the year when everything went horribly wrong. All the progress women had made in the last hundred years was all for nothing. The Republican-controlled Congress approved the twenty-week abortion ban, which began the quick descent into chaos.

President Rumba was assassinated along with Democratic nominees Dina Linton and Ernie Randers—all gunned down, their lives cut short because of their progressive political stances.

This happened in a supposed "Radical Socialist Attack," and most of America, even the Liberals, were willing to listen to the Radical Republicans. That was the biggest mistake of all.

The first order of business was to make abortion illegal. The circumstances under which a woman needs an abortion suddenly did not matter, the pregnancy was God's will. Shortly thereafter birth control and other forms of contraceptives were banned.

Women were fired and forced into jobs deemed more suitable for them (nursing, teaching, babysitting, etc.). They were prohibited from holding public office. Women could only read approved material deemed appropriate for their new, approved professions as mothers and housewives.

In this world, women's shorts and pants were banned. Dresses had to have elbow-length sleeves and knee-length hems, although floor-length was deemed ideal. Shoes had to be modest and comfortable. Girls didn't necessarily dress for comfort. They dressed to attract husbands. Purses and gloves had to be worn outside as was fashionable for women in the 1950's south. In fact, being from the South was the best attribute a woman can be.

Women older than I must look good for their husbands. You were put on earth to find a man. Ideally, you are slim with small breasts, average height, and perhaps, most disturbing of all white.

I fall into none of these categories. I am not of average height, I have large breasts, and curves. I was a misfit in a world where curves were a societal no-no. You do not want to entice men to rape you.

Women earn less than men, which wasn't a new development, just magnified. Now women make an average 45 cents an hour to a man's dollar. The government wants to ensure women have to marry men for survival. It's a patriarchal, contrived world where the "good ole' American life" has been interpreted at great cost to women. We are a subservient class, but then again we always were.

Chapter One

I awaken to the sound of broken glass. This is not uncommon where I live, a section of Los Angeles that may as well be a war zone. It's a part of town that at one time had numerous abortion clinics, and people in this section of the city fought hard to keep them.

But the "Baby Killer Riots of 2016" fueled a reversal of policies, with violent demonstrations that left this part of the city in shambles. The government did nothing to rebuild after the destruction. In fact, it served as a reminder—and a warning—of what happens when people defy the law.

We are forced to live in this section of the city because my mom and I cannot afford to live anywhere else. My mom is one of the few single mothers in this society. She had the nerve to leave my father and his abuse; something society chooses to ignore. Everything is a woman's fault, and if you do not keep your husband happy, your character is flawed. Almost universally, our neighbors are single parent families.

We are taught how to cook, clean, bake and make dresses. The only girls who get to take math and science are the ones who are becoming nurses or teachers.

I haven't quite figured out what I am going to do yet. I suck at making dresses, I don't like children, and I am mediocre at baking. Of course, I never dare to say any of this out loud. I could be taken away to a government facility where you are brainwashed to conform to societal norms.

"Mom, I'm leaving," I call.

"Okay, have a good day Neima," she responds.

I begin to walk the two blocks to school, streets with broken glass, drug needles and police everywhere. Law enforcement tends to be more prevalent in low-income neighborhoods because poor people are less likely to comply with gender roles than the wealthy. They can afford to do so; we can't.

The middle class and working poor keep the country afloat, paying most of the taxes. The wealthy one percent reaps the rewards of our hard work. The government continues to keep the rich happy because everyone else is either too scared or working themselves to death to fight. Even though most of the rich hate these policies, they don't want to stop making money; it's always about the money.

"Stop, young lady," I hear an officer yell.

I stop dead in my tracks. Running away from an officer could potentially leave a person dead. My mother's side of the family is originally from Israel. It's one of the reasons my father and mother got divorced— that and the physical abuse. My dad wanted to raise me Catholic with traditional gender roles.

My mom thought I had a right to choose what I wanted from life. Most people of my family are Jewish, but I do not have a religion. While agnosticism is not illegal, it is considered immoral, subject to apprehension for indecent behavior by the Moral Police. In general, people with no religion are harassed more by police. By attending temple, I dodge such suspicions. In the Unites States, any Protestant branch is preferred. The most moral of people are those who believe in a Christian God. If you are Catholic or Orthodox, the masses generally are likely to harass you, but it could be worse. Atheists can be hauled away on "moral grounds" if they cause too much trouble.

"State your name," the officer commands.

"Neima Levy."

My grandmother changed her last name to Levy upon entering the United States. I never asked her what her former name was.

"Where are you going?"

"I am going to school."

"Be careful, young lady."

"Will do, sir."

I continue walking until I arrived high school, through torn up streets and disheveled down buildings. During the riots, rioters broke windows and threw Molotov Cocktails, severely damaging many buildings. Like I said, the city won't fix or remove them. They are a grim and powerful reminder of past that government believes is valuable in shaping current public opinion. Huge sections of roadway are gone, destroyed by the heavy tanks used to quell the disturbances. Los Angeles has become the new Detroit.

I am a senior nearing graduation. I am quiet in school. I don't want to bring any unwanted attention to myself, though I tend to do that anyway. I have objects at home that I am not supposed to have—coveted music and books from "The Time of Feminism." I hide them beneath a loose floorboard under my bed. I have CDs, records, and books that could easily get me hauled away. My mother knows I have these things. She does not approve. Her advice: "Be careful."

In school, the girls are divided based on the type of husband they will marry. The girls who are white and Protestant marry rich white men. The girls who are not Protestant, but still white, usually marry middle-class husbands. Their classes are cooking, cleaning and housekeeping.

The non-Christians and non-white girls are going marry poor men. So we take classes in how to make clothes and cooking on a budget.

Wives with rich husbands are thin and of average height, with perfect hair, flawless skin, and no curves.

Prospective wives of middle-class men are a little shorter; they may have some acne, and they have some curves. They have small breasts and tiny butts.

Poor men have no other option that to marry girls who are on the short side with curves that rival those of Marilyn Monroe. They may have had skin problems in the past, but not now. They have a few scars. They go to classes with girls like them, except for baking class. Baking is mandated for every girl. Boys and girls are kept separate at all times, together only for sports games.

Boys are academically separated the same way we are. Boys who are white, tall and Protestant take classes in business and science to ensure they get high-paying jobs. They are what you stereotypically think of as all-American boys.

Down the social latter a tad, are males who are shorter but still Christian, and they take classes to become office managers and small business owners. Last on the academic ladder are minority boys who are short. They undoubtedly will find themselves slaving away in a white man's world.

I head to my first class—English. We are allowed to take that and social studies. In these categories, they teach us that being a strong, confident woman never ends well. History and literature are employed to enforce that view.

In English class, we are reading some book written in 1962 about how to be a good wife. It's called "The Good Wife: A Guide to Keeping Your Man Satisfied." I despise that book and the United States in general. But of course, I can't say that aloud.

I feel like screaming! It's not fair how women are expected to pop out babies and listen to men. It is not this way in other parts of the world. Women are allowed to have jobs, and they aren't expected to work for pennies. I want a life somewhere else, but the United States has the borders locked down to everyone but immigrants.

If you are an immigrant living here, you are allowed to leave to go back to your native country. US citizens have to sneak out over the borders, and the penalty for getting caught is twenty-five years in prison or a so-called "education" facility. My teacher, Mrs. Faye, begins to speak.

"What have you learned from the first two chapters, girls?" she asks.

"How to clean house," a girl says.

"Magnificent, Clara! Would anyone else like to share?"

Mrs. Faye scans the room.

"Niema, what have you learned?"

I think for a moment. I have to respond wisely. Everyone is watching.

"I found out that a woman must always listen and respect her husband."

"Excellent Niema. You have been paying attention."

I zone out for the rest of the period. I don't want to feed into the system any longer than I have to. The only thing you are allowed to listen to is Christian or other types of religious music. Everything else is banned. I hear the bell ring, and it is time to go to social studies. Today we are studying Joan of Arc and why she was foolish to think she could survive in a man's world. My teacher, Mrs. Harrison is even worse than Mrs. Faye with her anti-feminism bullshit.

"Okay, girls. Why could Joan of Arc never succeed in a man's world?" Mrs. Harrison asks.

A girl raises her hand.

"Women don't' belong in the military."

"Good job, Melanie. Anyone else?"

Everyone else remains silent.

"Come on, ladies. You must have learned something. I know we are not as smart as men, but you must have learned something, Niema, what about you?"

I guess today is my lucky day.

"A woman will never be successful in a man's world because we think with emotion and not logic."

"This is an excellent observation, Niema, but try not to sound too smart. Men don't appreciate it."

"Yes, ma'am."

That's another thing they teach us in school. Try to be smart, but not too smart. Men don't not like it. The girl's school day is shorter than men's because we are thought to have a shorter attention span. I don't mind. It gives me time to get a real education from my grandmother. My grandmother teaches me math and science when I go over to her house alone. The next class I have is dress making.

I suck at this course of study. I can fix garments, but I cannot make them. My partner has had to do most of the work. My partner Melanie and I are almost done. She is sewing the left side of the dress while I do the right. I can make small parts of the dress, but I cannot sew the actual dress itself.

"Good job, girls," Mrs. Myers says.

"Thank you," Melanie says.

"Thank you for helping me out with this," I mutter.

"It's my pleasure. I love making dresses," she says in an eerily sweet tone.

I finish sewing my sleeve on the dress, and I put my sewing supplies back. Melanie ends her side, and we are finally done with this dumb project.

"Are you a Jew?" Melanie asks in a disgusted tone.

"I practice the faith of Judaism, yes," I reply curtly.

The girls and Mrs. Myers are staring at me. I know I've said too much. I've been called down to the principal's office several times over this matter. I head to my next class, cooking on a budget. As soon as can walk into class, I can tell I am not going to be here long.

"Niema, the principal, would like to see you," Mrs. Dawson says.

"Okay," I say.

I head to the principal's office. He is male because, in a female dominated field, a man still has to be in charge. I knock on the door.

"Come in."

"You wanted to see me?"

"Yes, shut the door behind you."

I do what Mr. Ashburn asks.

"Mrs. Myers is worried that you are exerting too much knowledge in the classroom," Mr. Ashburn says.

The office looks like the place for a man who has something to prove. He has degrees from several colleges, including Columbia and Yale, on the wall. But this begs the question, what is he doing at a school in South Central Los Angeles? It's a typical principal's office, with a desk in the center and a chair directly behind it. The room is painted white and showing signs of age. It is in desperate need of a fresh coat.

"I didn't think I was," I say.

"Well, she expressed concern that you are."

"I don't know what to say."

"Well, I am going to send you home for the day."

"I understand."

"I will write you a note."

Women are not supposed to be outside without a purpose unless you are going somewhere essential such as school, work, grocery store or religious services. You must have a man with you or a note from a man granting you permission.

"Here you go."

I snatch the note from his hand, and I begin to walk home.

"Stop! What are you doing outside this time of day, young lady?" an officer asks.

I hand him the note. I know it says something about me being sent home for being too smart.

"Continue, and for the record, my wife is very dumb, and we have been happily married for twenty years."

"Good to know, sir," I say, holding back anger.

I continue to walk home, and I finally arrive there. Home, the only place where I can remain under the radar.

Chapter Two

I am in my room, listening to my forbidden music. It reminds me that there was a better life for women and a time when people dared to be different. When all non-religious music was banned, musical talent was given a choice—fade into obscurity or leave. Most artists left the United States, fleeing to either the United Kingdom or Germany.

The closest thing we have to a rock band now is Creed. I can't stand them. My mother has music from a few artists—Soundgarden, Nirvana, and L7—all artists from the 1990s. I believe this era was called grunge.

I wonder if the artists who fled the United States ever miss it here. And if so, why haven't they told anyone what's going on here? It's been ten years since this all started and I long for the days when I was a little kid and could wear whatever I wanted and walk around without a note. I hate this harsh life. I need more freedom! I don't want my room to be the only place where I feel free.

"Niema, come to the living room right now," my mother bellows!

I go down to the living room where my mom Isa awaits, hands on her hips. Great. This usually means I'm in for a lecture.

"What happened in school today?"

"I was sent home for being too smart again."

My mother sighs.

"Oh, honey, I wish you could show how smart you are, but girls who are too smart are taken away."

"I know, mom."

"I have seen what happens to those people. They are shells of their former selves."

My mother works at the hospital a couple of blocks away. I'm she sees these unfortunate souls all the time.

"I am trying to appear dumber, but it's harder than you think."

"Please do this for me. You already have a target on your back because of me."

"I am well aware of this," I say with a hint of anger in my voice.

I begin to walk back to my room when a thought crosses my mind. I turn back around.

"How did you know I was home?"

"The school called me."

It was signed into law that all men and women have religious holidays off. This is why my mother has Friday off, even though she should technically have Saturday off because Jews go to temple on Saturday morning. I head back into the shelter of my room, thankful for a little while that no one is watching me.

Mine is a single floor home. It's pleasant enough. Since no one wants to live here, we got it at a great price. We moved here when I was six, right after my parents split up. I haven't seen my father since, and he doesn't have to pay child support. It is a woman's job to raise children, not a man's. When a woman leaves her husband, she must pay child support. It's her duty to raise and care for her children. I hear a knock at the door.

"Come in," I say.

"It's time to go to temple," Isa says.

I grab my purse and gloves and head outside with my mother. My mother and I are the same height—five three. We have similar skin tones, but my mom is darker. Our eyes are brown. My hair is light brown; her's is black.

Temple is only a couple blocks away from home, and it's the one place I can go without being harassed.

"Hello to my two favorite girls."

"Hello, Grandma," I say, giving her a hug.

My grandma's name is Rivka. She is sixty-two years old and still full of piss and vinegar. Rivka is darker than my mom, but not by much. She has black hair that is beginning to gray, and she is the same height as my mother, and me.

"How is my granddaughter?" Rivka asks.

"Always getting into trouble as usual," Isa says.

"You're a Levy; it's what we do."

It's amazing after five decades after the United States Rivka still has a strong accent and a strong connection to her heritage.

"Why don't we find a seat," Isa says.

Rivka, Isa and I take a seat towards the front of temple. My grandmother told me recently she wants me to call her by her first name, as does my mother. They said it's a sign that I am becoming an adult in this family. I am not sure how I feel about that yet. Rabbi Feldman comes out.

"Everyone please sit down."

Everyone sits. In an Orthodox temple we would have to be separated from the men, but here we don't. Before we can start the service, we hear a heavy knocking on the temple door.

"Police! Open the door!"

A tiny old lady sitting towards the back opens the door.

"The mayor has banned all citywide religious services that are not Christian," An Officer tells us.

"He cannot do that," Rivka says.

"Yes, he can. According to penal code 99-2, the mayor may allow other religions to assemble as a privilege, not a right."

Everyone begins to leave the temple, and my grandmother attempts to walk home.

"Ma'am, you cannot go that way," an officer says.

"My home is that way," Rivka says.

"Rivka, knock it off and come back with us," Isa says slightly annoyed.

"I have a right to go to my home."

"Grandma, just spend the night with us, please. I will take you back in the morning," I plead with her.

Rivka gives up this fight and comes back with us.

"You know I asked you to call me Rivka," she says.

I remain silent. We arrive back at home.

"You can take my room Gr-Rivka."

"You are getting better at that, and I do not want to take your space."

"Don't be silly. I can live without my bed for just one night."

"Thank you, Niema. I want you to come home with me tomorrow."

"Okay. I thought we were done with my education," I whisper.

My mother doesn't know what my grandmother and I have been up to. I would like to keep it that way; she would surely disapprove.

"You are never done learning, my dear. And I have something I would like to give you."

"Okay, what is it?"

"You will see you tomorrow."

I head to my room and grab a pillow and blanket. I made up the couch. The furniture is a little busted and worn, but it serves its purpose.

"Good night," Isa says.

"Good evening, mo-Isa."

I fall asleep on the couch. When you live in this neighborhood, you get used to falling asleep to the sound of sirens, broken glass and sometimes, someone screaming. After a while, it becomes background noise. I wake up the next morning to the smell of eggs. I head to the kitchen.

"Good morning," Rivka says.

"Morning," I reply.

"I made you some eggs."

"Thank you. You didn't have to do that."

"I wanted to."

Rivka puts eggs on a plate, and we eat at the small kitchen table.

"How is school going?"

"Alright, I am not learning anything useful."

"You were sent home yesterday, weren't you?"

"Yes."

"What was it for this time?"

"Being too smart."

"What is this country coming to, where my granddaughter is sent home for being too smart," she says shaking her head in shame.

"It's not like I try to show it."

"You shouldn't have to hide anything."

"I know, but that's the way the world is."

I finish eating my breakfast and shower. The only good thing about this new world is that utility bills are cheap. Everything else is awful. I take a quick shower and change my clothes.

"Are you ready to go?" Rivka asks.

"Yes."

I walk with my grandmother to her house.

"Where are you going?" An officer asks.

"My granddaughter is coming home with me to assist me in some tasks," Rivka says.

"Okay, make sure you are home by sunset," the officer says.

"Yes sir," I say.

We continue to my grandmother's house. My grandma lives in a tiny house in a slightly nicer part of the city. Resources can sometimes be a little scarce due to the increasing droughts, but everyone pools them together to survive. We arrive at my grandmother's house.

My grandmother's house is one floor just like mine, except she has another bedroom where she stores arts and crafts. My grandmother owned an arts and crafts store until they banned all women from owning businesses. She was forced to sell the place. Now she lives off the money from the sale of the shop and my grandfather's pension.

My grandfather worked as a corrections officer, but he quit right after they outlawed women from working in certain fields. He didn't think it was fair my grandmother had to stay home all day, and he could work.

Although my grandmother and mother look alike, their personalities could not be more different. My grandmother is brazen, and my mom is meek. My mom is quiet and does not like to bring attention to herself. My grandmother is loud, daring and draws attention to herself wherever she goes.

"Niema," Rivka says.

"Yes," I say, lost in my thoughts.

"Follow me."

I follow Rivka to her bedroom and watch ads she digs through her jewelry box. My grandmother gives me a necklace; it's the Star of David.

"My grandmother gave me this necklace when I was your age. I know that you do not follow the faith, but this is an heirloom that has been passed down from grandmother to granddaughter for generations. So please humor your dear old grandmother."

"I will."

I put the necklace on.

"I am so proud of you."

"I haven't done anything for you to be proud of yet."

"You are smart and confident. I know you will do something great."

"I am not so sure about that."

"I know you will. You should go home before the officers haul you off to jail or worse."

"I love you, Rivka."

Rivka gives me a kiss, and I begin to head home.

* * *

"Where are you going, young lady?" an officer asks.

"Home," I say.

"What are you doing out?"

"I was at my grandmother's house helping her clean."

The officer looks down at me, which at his height of six-four isn't hard to do.

"Are you a Jew?" he asks pointing to the necklace.

"Yes," I say innocently.

"You cannot practice in the city anymore. Maybe now you will find the light of Christ."

"If I remember correctly, Christ was a Jew."

"What did you say?"

The officer grabs my wrist and tightens his grip.

"You can't hit a lady officer…unless she is your wife, of course."

He lets me go, and I quickly head home. Until women are married, they are the property of their fathers, and police officers are not allowed to hit them. As soon as they get married, they are the property of their husbands, and subject to beating as often as he likes. I open the door to my home, and I lock it behind me.

What the hell was I thinking? I can't talk to the cops like that. They could have beaten me with the nightstick, shot me or worse. They could have dragged me to any number of facilities. I have to watch how I act. I hear a knock on the door. I open it. It's Isa.

"Why did you lock all of the locks?" Isa asks.

"An officer harassed me on my way home," I reply.

"Maybe you shouldn't wear that necklace."

"Why shouldn't I?"

"Because the harassment of Jews is only getting worse. The only group target-ed more than we are is Muslims, and we both know why that is."

"Yes I do, but someone has to stand up to the system if things are ever to change."

"Niema, don't stir the pot."

"I don't mean to."

"Please don't get taken away to one of those facilities."

"I won't.

I get ready for bed, and as I do, I think about the person I want to become. Do I want to be a housewife who only dreams of a better life and waits for someone else to make things happen? Or do I want to be the woman making that happen?

Chapter Three

My mom leaves for work early the next morning. I stay in bed. My mom has to be home before nightfall. We never know what might happen to us after dark. I decide to relax today; I have to stay at school late tomorrow because I am a part of the flag organization at school. Whenever the boys have a football game or basketball game, all of the organizations have to get together and support the men. My job as part of the flag club is to dress up in a red, white and blue dress and hold up the flag, along with two other girls. Pro-American values are important.

This is the only club where you have to meet on the day of the games. Cheerleading is the only "sport," we are allowed to participate in. Tomorrow in school I won't have class. I will just have to set up for the basketball game. While a lot of people like basketball, it is still football that reigns supreme at my school and in America.

I wake the next morning with a sense of dread. I loathe doing these kinds of things. The men get to be heroes, and the girls have to stand on the sidelines and wait to be rescued. This morning I put on my red, white, and blue dress, with my matching shoes and bag.

"Isa, I'm leaving."

"Wait; I'm almost ready."

I watch my mother come around the corner.

"Are you prepared to go?"

"Yes."

We leave the house, and my mother begins to walk with me. My high school is a straight two blocks from my house while my mom has to take a right at the end of our block.

The nursing uniform my mother wears looks similar to those in the 1950s. The only difference is now they are made of lighter material.

Nurses are required to wear white. In other professions, men and women are expected to wear bright colors at all times. Black is never to be worn unless you are going to a funeral or in mourning. Black is associated with the devil and times of grief. Red would be, too, but red is one of the colors of the American flag.

"See you after the game, sweetie."

"See you later Isa."

I continue to head off to school, and as I do, I receive strange looks. I shrug it off. It's probably because of the necklace. I keep walking until I reach school. I head straight to the gym to help with setting up.

"Hello, Niema."

"Hello, Meghan."

"Can you help Katherine set up the flags on the wall?"

"Sure."

I put my purse on the bleachers, and I climb the ladder to help Katherine pin the flag to the wall. We have the flag in place in no time. As soon as I climb down, someone grabs me and puts a black bag over my head. It's the Moral's Police! What the hell do they want with me?! I haven't done anything wrong! I behave myself! I do everything I can so this doesn't happen! What have I done wrong?

I feel myself being lifted off the ground to what I am assuming is a police van. People taken away by the Moral's Police are too dangerous to be put with common criminals. I hear the door close. We drive for about forty-five minutes. The van comes to a hard, abrupt stop. I am ripped from the forced into a building.

Once I am inside, the hood is taken off. I am in jail. It could be worse. I could be at one of those facilities. I am brought down a flight of stairs and led from blinding light into darkness. They force me into a cell and lock the door.

"Why am I here?" I ask.

Silence.

"Why am I here?" I ask again.

The Moral's Police begin to walk away.

"Hey, come back here! I have a right to know why I am here! Get back here! I know my rights!" I say, slamming on the bars.

I continue screaming for half an hour. I stop when I realize it's futile. How did I end up in jail? Did someone turn me in? If so, then who? It doesn't matter now.

I hear the door open at the end of the hallway, and I turn around. A woman with a cart is making her way down the row of cells. The woman gets to me. She stops.

"You have quite the pair of lungs on you," the woman says. She speaks with an accent.

My ears perk up. We don't have a lot of young or middle-aged immigrants living in America anymore. When the laws were passed, most of them went back to their native countries.

"I guess so," I whisper.

"We could hear you all the way upstairs."

"I'm sorry."

"Don't be. Most people who come in here are too afraid to stand up for their rights."

"It does not appear to be doing me a lot of good."

The woman hands me a cup of water and a plate.

"I'm Malene."

"Niema."

"You should eat and save your strength; you are going to need it."

I sit down on the long metal bench and open the cover to the plate. The meal is overcooked chicken with undercooked rice. I drink the water, but I don't touch the food. The woman comes back, and I hand her the plate.

"Get your rest; you're going to need that, too."

I lie down on the bench, but I do not get much sleep. The seat is cold, and so is my cell. The next morning I hear footsteps coming downstairs.

"Levy, up," a guard demands.

I slowly get up from the bench. The guards open the door, and he grabs my arm...HARD!

"Do you think this is funny Jew?"

"A little bit," I say amused.

The guard leads me upstairs through the front part of the building. The guard stops in front of what appears to be an interview room. He throws me into the chamber. Inside, there's a young man with bright blonde hair, blue eyes. He looks to be around sixteen.

"How old are you?" I ask instinctively.

"I am twenty-seven years old."

I sit down at the table, which looks like a cafeteria table from when I was a kid.

"Why am I here?"

"You have been accused of being too smart, and the state has a strong case against you."

"What is your strategy to get me out of here?"

"You let me worry about that."

"What is the plan?!" I demand.

"Part of the problem is that you are too smart, and I can see that. I need you for this trial to play dumb and to take off that necklace."

"That is your plan for me, to play stupid?"

"Trust me. I am a man. I know what I am doing."

"You could have fooled me."

My lawyer does not look amused.

"When does the trial start?" I ask, trying to break the tension in the air.

"Tomorrow."

"Does my family know I'm here?"

"Yes, and I have to say your family situation is not helping you. Do you know where your father is?"

"No."

"Do you have any way to contact him?"

"No."

I watch the lawyer take notes.

"That is all I need to know."

"What happens if you lose this trial for me?"

"Don't think about that."

"It's my ass on the line."

The lawyer leaves, and I am lead back to my cell. I have no idea what time it is. There are no clocks, and I cannot see the sun. I hear someone open the door at the end of the row.

"Dinner time," I listen to the same woman from last night say.

It's difficult to see down here with the lack of light unless something or someone is right in front of you.

"I am surprised you are still here," Malene says in a lively tone.

"My trial starts tomorrow," I reply weakly.

"Good luck."

"Thank you."

I look at the women carefully. She has dark brown hair, blue eyes, and very pale white skin. She is two inches taller than me.

"Here is your dinner and drink."

"Thank you."

"You're welcome."

I open the plate cover. Tonight, it is one of those frozen TV dinners that has been left in the microwave a little too long. I decide to eat. I don't know when I may eat again. Dinner isn't terrible, but it is not great either. I give the plate and cup to Malene.

"Good luck tomorrow."

When Malene leaves, I lie down on the bench, and I think about the future. The future definitely doesn't look too bright right now.

Chapter Four

"Levy, up," I hear a guard say.

I get up off the bench, and the guard leads me upstairs. A bag is put over my head again. I am led to a van, and it begins to move. A few hours later, it stops. Again, I am led out of the vehicle and into a building. Once inside, the bag is taken off. The building is a courthouse, and everyone is looking at me. I guess it's not every day a woman is brought to court by the Moral's Police.

"I will take it from here, officers," my lawyer says.

The police let me go, and I walk with my attorney. I realize in all that time I spent with him yesterday, I never bothered to learn about him.

"What's your name?"

"David," he says, a little annoyed.

David has bright blonde hair and blue eyes. He is six-foot-two with a stocky build. He is the perfect all-American male complete with a pale complexion.

"How will this trial work?"

"Well, first things first. You need to clean yourself up."

He hands me a bag containing clothes.

"At the end of the hall, there is a shower. Use that, clean yourself up, and put some makeup on."

I grab the bag and head to the shower. I take a quick shower and change into the dress David brought. It is a dark blue dress almost a little too long for me. I emerge from the shower room.

"Why no makeup?" David asks.

"I suck at putting it on."

"You're not helping your case."

"Why are there showers in a courthouse?" I ask, trying to change the subject.

"People arrested by the Moral's Police go to a different jail; those happen to have no showers."

We head into a courtroom. The prosecution's attorney is already here. He is a stern looking man in his fifties with gray hair and brown eyes. He is slightly taller than David, making him six-foot-four.

"Hello, David," the attorney says.

"Hello, Arthur," David responds.

I say nothing and sit down. I feel someone tap me on the shoulder. It is Rivka, with Isa standing next to her.

"Fancy meeting you here," Rivka says.

"What are you doing here?" I ask surprised.

"You're my daughter. You need me. How could you think I wouldn't be here?" Isa asks.

"I didn't want you to see me like this," I say, ashamed.

"Why not? I am proud of you right now," Rivka says.

"Thank you," I reply, trying to sound upbeat.

David comes over to the table.

"Are you her mother and grandmother?" he asks whispering.

"Yes I am, Isa Levy, and this is my mom Rivka," they whisper.

"Pleased to meet you both. I am going to call you as character witnesses."

"Okay," Isa says.

"Alright, now I need to ask you a few questions."

"Ask away," Rivka says.

"Now you are both American citizens, correct?"

"Yes," Rivka responds.

"And how long have you been in the United States, Mrs. Levy?"

"Fifty-seven years."

"And where are you originally from?"

"Israel."

"Okay, and Ms. Levy, how long have you been divorced?"

"Twelve years."

"And who started the paperwork."

"I did."

"Okay. Try to avoid mentioning these things on the stand."

"All rise for the honorable Judge Pitts."

Everyone stands; Rivka and Isa return to their seats.

"Please sit."

The judge is another stern-looking man in his fifties with gray hair and blue eyes that seemed to peer right into my soul.

"Okay, I call this case to order. The State of California versus Niem Levy."

That is not my name, but I let it go.

"Is the prosecution ready to proceed?"

"Yes your honor," the lawyer says with confidence. He looks cocky and as if he is about to destroy me, which he probably is.

"Is the defense ready to proceed?"

"Yes your honor," he says in a polite tone.

"Is the state ready to call its first witness?"

"Yes, your honor. The state would like to call Melanie Smith to the stand."

Melanie walks from her spot that was in the back of the room. She is dressed in a plain white dress with matching shoes and gloves. Her skin is a little lighter than mine, and she has straight, dirty blonde hair and piercing blue eyes. I think Melanie is mixed. Her mom is white, and her father is Puerto Rican.

I tap my lawyer on the shoulder.

"What about opening statements?" I ask.

"Those are optional," he replies.

"Would you please state your name for the court?" the opposing attorney asks.

"My name is Melanie Fernandez."

"And do you attend high school with the defendant?"

"Yes I do," she says with confidence.

"What is the Niema personality?"

"Objection, your honor. Opinion. This witness is not an expert, and therefore, cannot give an opinion."

"Objection is overruled. The witness may answer."

"Would you like me to repeat the question?"

"No. Niema is a bit odd. She does not talk a lot, and she does not have a boyfriend."

"And why is that?"

"I am not sure, but the rumor around school is that she likes women and not men," Melanie says with a wicked smile on her face.

I hear gasps from the courtroom, sounds that seem to have come straight from a soap opera.

"Objection, your honor. I move to have that stricken from the record," David says with a fiery passion.

"So ordered. Watch it, Arthur," Judge Pitts says in a strict tone.

"Yes, your honor. Does the defendant participate in class?" he asks in an oddly charming way.

"Yes, and she has a very, um…," Melanie says with a confused look on her face.

She cannot think of the word.

"Extended vocabulary."

"What does that mean?" she asks with a blank look on her face.

"She knows a lot of big words."

"Yes and she sounds very…"

"Sophisticated?" the attorney says.

"What does that mean?" she asks, looking more confused than before.

"She sounds smart." the attorney says, annoyed.

"Oh, yes she does.'"

"Are there any other rumors about the defendant?"

"Objection, your honor, Hearsay. We don't know where this information is coming from," David says sounding very annoyed.

"Overruled. The witness may answer the question," the judge says nonchalantly.

"Yes. She enjoys reading banned books and listening to forbidden music. That's how she knows all of those big words," Melanie says, looking straight at me with an evil grin.

I hear more whispering and gasps coming from the gallery.

"Order in the court," Judge Pitts says, banging the gavel angrily.

"No further questions, your honor," the attorney says smugly.

"David, your witness."

"Did you ever see my client reading these banned books or listening to this forbidden music?" David asks?

"No."

"And isn't it possible my client paid attention in class, and that is why she is smarter than you."

"I guess so," she says looking defeated.

"And how well do you know my client?"

"I don't know her at all," she says with less confidence than she did earlier.

"No further questions, your honor."

"The witness may step down. Call your next witness."

"The people call Beatrice Harrison to the stand."

I watch my teacher take her position in the witness box. I knew there was a reason I never liked her.

"Mrs. Harrison, how long have you been a teacher?"

"Thirty years."

"And do you have the defendant as a student?"

"Yes, I do."

"And how would you describe her?"

"Odd. She does enjoy learning, and she does not want to find a husband."

"And how would you describe her intelligence?"

"Above average; it's almost as if someone taught her at home."

I hear loud gasps and people speaking out of outrage.

"Order in the court," Judge Pitts barks, banging the gavel.

"Objection, your honor. I move to strike that from the record."

"I will disregard that statement."

"Does the defendant seem interested in women's pursuit?"

"No."

"Does she like to read?"

"Yes."

"Thank you, Mrs. Harrison. No further questions."

"Your witness, David."

"Mrs. Harrison, do you have any evidence has been taught at home?"

"No."

"Thank you. No further questions, your honor."

"You may step down, Mrs. Harrison. Is the state ready to call its final witness?"

"Yes. The state would like to call Burt Ashburn."

Principal Ashburn is a balding man in his forties with an ugly beer gut and pale skin.

"You may be seated."

"Mr. Ashburn, how long have you been a principal?"

"Sixteen years."

"And has the defendant ever been to your office?"

"Yes."

"What has she been called to your office for?"

"Complaints about her being too smart and that she does not engage in typical women's pursuits."

"Could you give us an example?"

"She does not like making dresses, cooking or finding husbands."

"How many times has the defendant been called to your office this year?"

"Several."

"No further questions, your honor."

"Your witness, David."

"You aren't sure how many times my client has been in your office, are you?"

"No."

"And has my client been called into your office for anything violent?"

"No."

"Thank you. No further questions, your honor."

"You may step down, Mr. Ashburn. I am going to call a half hour recess."

The judge bangs his gavel, and I quickly head to the bathroom. With my dark blue dress, white stockings, white shoes and white gloves, I look pure and innocent. I hope that is enough to get me off. I head back to the courtroom. A moment ago it was thunderous and chatty. As soon as I enter, it becomes mute. All eyes are on me. I head back to the table and sit down. Isa and Rivka come down to the table.

"What is the plan?"

"I am going to call your grandmother to the stand, then your mother and then you."

"Okay."

"Oh, and on the stand try not to sound smart."

"I will try not to, good sir."

"All rise for the honorable Judge Pitts."

Everybody rises as the judge walks back in.

"Please sit down. Are the people ready to proceed?"

"Yes, your honor."

"Is the defense ready?"

"Yes, your honor."

"Are you ready to call your first witness?"

"Yes, your honor. The defense calls Rivka Levy to the stand."

I watch my grandmother takes her position on the witness stand. She doesn't look the least bit nervous.

"Mrs. Levy, how often are you around your granddaughter?" David asks in a polite tone.

"I am with her once a week, sometimes more," my grandmother says in her usual confident tone.

"And how smart is she?"

"She is not smarter than the average girl."

I flinch a little bit when she says that. I know it killed her to make such a statement.

"And have you ever taught her anything that would be against the law?"

"No."

"Thank you, Mrs. Levy. No further questions, your honor."

"Your witness, Arthur."

"Are you Jewish Mrs. Levy?" the opposing attorney asks in a cocky tone.

"Objection, your honor. Relevancy. What does her religion have to do with the trial?" David says with a slight hint of defeat in his voice.

"Overruled. The witness may answer," Judge Pitts says.

"Yes I am," my grandmother says proudly.

"And are you initially from this country?" the attorney asks with a hint of hate in his voice.

"No, I am from Israel."

"And how long have you been in this country?" he asks with the hatred in his voice more evident now.

"I have been here for fifty-seven years," my grandmother says with pride.

"Thank you. No further questions, your honor."

"You may step down, Mrs. Levy. Are you ready to call your next witness?

"Yes, your honor. The defense calls Isa Levy to the stand."

My mother takes the stand.

"Ms. Levy, what do you do for a living?"

"I'm a nurse."

"So you spend your day saving lives?"

"Yes."

"And how often are you home?"

"I leave a little after my daughter in the morning, and I am always home by dark."

"Have you ever seen Niema reading something she shouldn't be?"

"No."

"Thank you. No further questions, your honor."

"Your witness, Arthur."

"Ms. Levy, are you divorced?"

"Yes, I am."

"And who started that process?"

"I did officially after my daughter's father choked me so hard I passed out."

"And how long ago was that?"

"Twelve years ago."

"And are you Jewish?"

"Yes."

"Thank you. No further questions, your honor."

"You may step down, Ms. Levy. Is the defense ready to call their final witness?"

"Yes, your honor. The defense calls Niema Levy to the stand."

I walk to the witness box, and the courtroom suddenly becomes silent. I could hear a pin drop right now.

"Ms. Levy, how old are you?"

"I am seventeen years old."

"And what do you like to do?"

"I like to cook and read the books that we are assigned to in school," I say in the sweetest tone possible.

"What about dress making?"

"Oh, I am not magnificent at that, but I always try my best, and I am good at fixing them," I say, sounding as dumb as possible.

"That is quite alright. Many people are bad at making them. Are you Jewish, Ms. Levy?"

"Yes, I am."

"And have you in any way violated the law stating Jews can no longer practice in Los Angles?"

"No."

"And have you ever been taught at home anything that would violate the law?"

"No."

"Thank you. No further questions, your honor."

"Your witness, Arthur."

"Ms. Levy, can you do math?"

"No."

"Do you know what multiplication is?"

24

"No."

"Can you make a dress?"

"I can fix them; I am not splendid at making them."

"Have you ever been taught at home?"

"My mother tried to teach me how to sew at home, does that count?"

"I meant anything illegal?" he asks clearly annoyed.

"No."

"Thank you. No further questions, your honor."

I return to the table.

"I will not hear closing arguments. I will now retire to my chambers to consider the defendant's fate."

The judge rises from the bench and leaves the room.

"Good job on the stand," David says proudly.

"Thanks, I thought the judge was supposed to hear closing arguments."

"That is optional."

Isa and Rivka walk over to the table.

"What is the judge going to do?" Isa asks.

"I am not sure. It could go either way."

"What is my granddaughter facing if she is found guilty?" Rivka asks sounding nervous.

"Jail or she may be sent to an education center."

"And how long will I be there if I'm locked up?"

"Until the courts decide you can leave."

"All rise for the honorable Pitts."

Isa and Rivka go back to their seats. This judge was gone all of ten minutes. What's the rush?

"Will the defendant rise?"

David and I rise.

"Niem Levy, I find you guilty of being too bright, and I order you to the Alvarez Education Center until you can eliminate this undesirable behavior."

The judge bangs the gavel, and I feel someone grab my arm. My worst nightmare has come true.

Chapter Five

When did I suddenly become like a dangerous armed criminal? Why am I here?! The only sound I heard on the drive to the facility was the sound of shackles clinking; mine and those around me. To the public, these are the facilities where no one wants to be. Officially, they are education centers designed to teach young women to behave. However, rumors swirl of young girls being abused at these centers.

One by one, we are led out of the van and into the facility. The building is nice looking. It has modern features and shows signs of being renovated in the last few years. I have a feeling, though, that something dark lurks just below the surface. I think I've read about this building in a book. It used to be an asylum for the criminally insane in the late 1800s, and early 1900s.

I hear the sound of boots on the floor. A middle-aged woman in a long navy blue skirt and blue blouse appears. She has close-cropped blonde hair and blue eyes, another gaze that seems to peer straight into your soul.

"You can unshackle them now," the woman says.

The guards do as she says.

"My name is Anne Alvarez, and I am in charge of this facility. As long as you can follow the rules, which we will go over tomorrow, you will be just fine."

No one says anything.

"My family has been operating this place for more than a hundred years. We will turn you into proper young ladies. Now rest, tomorrow will be an exciting day for you all."

The guards lead us all into different directions; I am led straight down a hallway. We stop when we reach the last door at the end. The guard leads me inside, and he points me to bed that is empty. I head to the bed, the guard unshackles me and leaves. I lie down, and I try to sleep. But sleep eludes me, so I stare at the wall.

"Why were you sent here?" a female voice asks.

I turn to see a young woman in the bed next to mine. She is wearing a long gray dress, and she has long brown hair, brown eyes, and medium skin tone.

"I was found guilty of being too smart. What about you?" I ask.

"I ran away from my wedding," she replies.

"And you were caught?"

"Yes, my name is Emily Reynolds."

"Niema Levy."

"Is that a Jew name?" she asks, surprised.

"Yes, what is this place like?"

"They try to brainwash you into thinking your purpose in life is to keep your husband happy and pop out babies."

"Oh joy, how long have you been here?"

"I've been here for five months."

"When do you get to leave?"

"When my fiancée decides I am a loving wife who won't run away from him. What about you?"

"When it is determined I am no longer intelligent."

"Have fun with that."

"Thanks."

I don't sleep that night. I hear the sound of a bell the next morning.

"Niema, it's time to get up," Emily says.

I wake up and follow Emily to where breakfast is served. I pick up an apple and sit down at the table next to her.

"What happens to me today?" I ask.

"They strip you of your identity, and they give you this lovely dress," Emily says, pointing to the one she has on.

"Oh how beautiful," I say sarcastically.

I hear a door open.

"All new arrivals come with me now," a woman says.

"Good luck," Emily says.

"Thanks," I reply.

I walk away with the other new girls. We are led down the hall to a white room. Anne is there waiting.

"Alright, ladies, take your dresses and jewelry off.

We all look at each other.

"Don't just look at each other; do it now!"

We all do as we were told, and we look at each other awkwardly.

"You are probably wondering why we are doing this. You must be stripped of your identity before we can rebuild you as respectable ladies of your society."

I look around at the other entire group of young girls shivering.

"Are you ready to become the proper young ladies we all know you can be?"

We all nod.

"Alright, bring the clothes in."

A band of young women brings in gray dresses, and we change into these ugly things.

"Are you ready to start your new life?"

I nod, and so does everyone else; play the game and get out of here.

"Good. I'm glad so you see things my way."

The young women gather our clothes and jewelry.

"When you start to behave, you will get your personal effects back. Take them back to their rooms. You begin learning tomorrow."

A few more employees come in, and I am lead out of the room by a middle-aged man. He has black hair, blue eyes and he is five-foot-ten with pale skin. The man leads me back to my room. Emily is here.

"How do you feel?" Emily asks.

"I feel like shit," I reply.

"Don't worry. Unless you cause a lot of trouble, they don't employ the more extreme methods."

"What are the extreme methods?"

"Solitary confinement, waterboarding, things that are not ethical."

"Good to know."

We hear a knock at the door.

"Who is it?" Emily asks.

"It's Hans. I need Ms. Levy."

I go to the door.

"What am I needed for? "I ask.

"You have a visitor."

I follow Hans down the hallway, and I recognize him as the middle-aged man from earlier. I am expecting to see my mother or grandmother, but it's not either of them. I walk into the room to find my long-lost father. What the fuck does he want?! I haven't seen him since I was a kid! Anne is already in the room.

"Thank you, Hans, I can take it from here," Anne says.

"Hello Neima," he says kindly.

"Hello Walter," I say with no humor in my voice.

I sit down at the table across from my father.

"Can you call me Dad?"

"I don't know can you not disappear for twelve years?"

"I understand you're mad, but I came here to talk to you."

I look at my father with this green eyes, bleached blonde hair and pale white skin. He is six-feet tall and muscular. We look nothing alike, and I am grateful for that now.

"What do you want?"

"When this is all over, I want you to come live with me."

"Why would you want that?" I ask shocked.

"My wife agreed to let you live with us, and she will teach you how to be a proper young lady."

"I'm listening," I say half-heartedly.

"You could meet your brother and sister, and I would be more than happy to help you find a husband."

"Do my brother and sister know that they have an older sister?

"No."

"Right. I forgot I am your shameful secret."

"Niema, do not talk like that!" he snaps.

"I have no desire to join your other family. I am going back to my mother."

"I should have known that leaving you with your mom you would end up like this."

"What a strong independent woman she is! Your manly mind can't handle that?" I ask holding back no anger.

"I see this isn't going anywhere."

"Do you abuse your new wife like you did mom?"

Walter leaves, and Anne sits down at the table.

"That was rude," Anne says in a superior tone.

"I was telling him the truth."

"You will never find a husband acting that way."

"Who says I want one."

"We have a lot of work to do with you. Hans take the girl back to her room."

Hans comes in, and he escorts me back to my room.

"My name is Hans Arentz."

"Niema Levy."

"Try to keep your head down during your time here."

"Will do."

I head back into my room.

"Who came to visit you?"

"My sperm donor."

"Who?"

"My father."

"Oh, and how did that go?" she asks sarcastically.

"I told him what I thought of him."

"You've got guts. I'll give you that."

"Thanks."

"You will need guts to make it through here."

I hear the bell ring.

"It's dinner time."

I follow Emily to the cafeteria. I grab a piece of chicken and sit down.

"Is your mom a single parent?"

"Yes."

"Did your father leave her?"

"My mom filed for divorce after he choked her so hard she passed out."

"Wow, that is ballsy."

"My father is a unique piece of shit. Are your parents still together?"

"Yes, they live in Paonia."

I finish my chicken, and I feel someone grab me.

"What is going on?" I ask.

A couple of guards grab my arms. No one says anything as I am dragged into a white room. I am put on a table and strapped in. Then these round metal things are put on my head.

"I am doing this for your sake Niema," Anne says.

I hear something switch on. An unbearable pain moves from my head down to my toes. All I feel is pain and light headedness. My vision is blurry, and I can't move. Light is the last thing I see before I pass out.

Chapter Six

"Niema! Niema!" I hear someone call as they shake me.

I turn over in bed. I see Emily and Hans.

"What happened to me?" I ask weakly.

"You were given ECT treatment," Hans explains.

"How long have I been out?" I ask, rubbing my head.

"Three days," Emily says.

"Ow!"

"How do you feel?"

"I feel like someone ran me over with a truck."

"Do you feel well enough to stand up?"

I try to stand up, and I fall right back on the bed.

"Niema!"

"I will tell Anne that she is still feeling ill."

I fall onto the bed.

"Niema!" Emily says shaking me.

"I'm up!"

"How do you feel?"

"I feel slightly better."

"Good you should shower before class."

I quickly shower, and I change into a new gray dress. I walk out of my room to find Hans standing outside the door.

"Am I in trouble again?"

"No, I've been tasked with shadowing you."

I walk with Emily and Hans, and I wait until I am in line with Emily and Hans is not around me before speaking again.

"What's the deal with Hans?"

"He's cool; you can trust him."

"Are you sure?"

"Yes, he stayed by your side the entire time you were passed out."

"That was sweet of him."

"He was worried about you."

I grab some food and sit down with Emily and Hans. We have breakfast before class begins.

"What kind of courses will I take here?"

"For you probably how to apply makeup and how to act like a woman."

"Oh, joy."

"You will survive."

"You have ten more minutes to eat, girls," a woman says.

"Didn't we just get here?"

"They don't like you to have a lot of free time together," Hans says.

I remain silent for a moment. This is the first time I've listened to Hans talk, and I realize he has a slight accent.

"Hans is a German name, is it not?"

"Yes, it is also Danish and Dutch, along with a few others."

"Girls, it's time to go," a staff member says.

I follow Hans down a short walkway to another white room. The girls I arrived with are also here.

"Please sit down in front of the mirror."

I do as I'm told. A woman walks into the room. She is five-foot-ten with long blonde hair and hazel eyes. She appears to be in the early twenties.

"My name is Ms. Linda, and I am here to make sure you can apply makeup correctly. Now put the foundation on.

This class makes me nervous. I taught myself how to do makeup, but I've never had anyone tell me if I've ever done it correctly.

"Did anyone ever teach you how to do makeup?"

"No, I taught myself."

"Well, good job."

"Thank you."

I hear the door open, and I turn around to see who it is. It's Anne.

"Okay, good job ladies. Now put on some mascara and lipstick.

I do the first two things with ease.

"Wow, girls! You're doing great. One last thing for today, I want you to put eyeliner on."

I put the eyeliner on the best I can, but it looks askew.

"Do you think this is funny, Ms. Levy?" Anne asks.

"No I was never taught how to do makeup," I say in my sweetest voice.

"She's been fantastic, Ms. Alvarez. She has been doing an incredible job today in class."

"Guards, take her away!"

I feel a man throw me over his shoulders while another man follows close behind. I am brought to a white room, where my arms and feet are bound to a chair.

"What are we going to do with you, Ms. Levy," Anne says walking around in a circle.

"You could let me be myself."

Anne laughs in an evil and menacing way.

"Oh, Ms. Levy. You are funny."

Anne approaches me with a nightstick in her hand. This is not looking good.

"What is the nightstick for?"

"You will find out."

Anne walks around me in a circle a couple of times, and then I feel something hit my feet. It does not register for a few moments that I have been struck in the foot. I don't scream, but it is hard not to.

"What was that for?" I ask through the pain.

"When you break the rules there are consequences."

I feel the nightstick come down again, this time with more force. I resist the urge to scream but this time, it's a lot harder.

I feel the nightstick strike me again. She puts all of her might into it. I manage not to scream, but it is very hard. I look down at my feet. They are black and blue and covered in blood.

"Let this be a reminder of what happens when you defy the rules."

Anne walks away and goes to the intercom.

"Hans, get the girl."

Hans comes into the room, and he looks appalled by what he sees.

"What have you done?" Hans asks horrified.

"I am trying to turn this unruly young girl into a proper young lady."

"Well, beating her isn't the way to do it!"

"Fear is a great way to get what you want. Now take her back to her room. Now!"

Hans unties me from the chair, puts me in a wheelchair and wheels me back to my room. Hans lifts me up and lowers me gently back onto the bed.

"I'll be right back."

I can't move it hurts too much. Hans comes back to my room.

"I am going to try to stop the bleeding and clean your wound."

"Okay."

Hans puts a towel on my feet, and he squeezes.

"Ow," I say.

"I'm sorry."

"It's not your fault."

I hear Emily enter the room.

"Oh my god! What happened?"

"Anne beat her with a nightstick."

"Why?"

"Because I am bad at putting on makeup, and she sees this as a threat to her power."

"She did a number on your feet."

"It hurts to move them."

"This is going to hurt for a bit. Emily, can you help me wrap her feet?"

"Of course, I can."

I watch Emily and Hans wrap my feet up, and I struggle not to cry out. I know they are just trying to help me, but why does this have to hurt so much.

"We are almost done, Niema. I'm sorry. I know this hurts," Hans says.

"It's not your fault."

Emily and Hans finish wrapping my feet.

"Do you know how to use a wheelchair?"

I nod.

"Okay, good."

Hans hands me a box.

"These have makeup wipes in them, wipe your face off."

Emily hands me a mirror, and I wipe my face.

"I have to go. I will see you tomorrow."

"Good night Hans."

I lie back down on the bed, and I wonder if I will ever be free again.

Chapter Seven

Getting my clothes on proves to be a challenge. Rolling the white stockings over my feet hurts like hell. Despite the pain, I cannot afford to forget them. It hurts, even more, to put on the dress. I can only stand for a few seconds before the pain begins to envelop me. I quickly put on the dress and get back into the wheelchair. I look at the shoes I have to put on. They are flat, and they don't fit me. My feet are too swollen.

"Good morning, Neima."

"Morning, Hans. Where is Emily?"

"I am not sure. Would you like me to get you a different pair of shoes?" he asks looking down at my feet.

"Yes, please."

Hans leaves the room, and he comes back with slightly bigger shoes.

"These look more your size."

"Thank you."

"You're welcome."

I wheel myself to the cafeteria where Hans grabs breakfast for me—a banana and some toast.

"Thank you."

"It's my job."

"How long have you been in the United States?"

"I've been here for twenty-five years."

"Do you ever want to go back home?"

"I have unfinished business here."

I eat the rest of my breakfast in silence.

"Girls, it is time to go to class," a woman calls.

Hans throws the plate away, and I wheel myself to makeup class. I am one of the first ones there. The teacher, Ms. Linda, looks at me oddly.

"Niema you are no longer in here," she says.

"Where am I supposed to go?" I ask.

"You are coming with me," Anne says.

I don't see Anne, but I know she is the one pushing the wheelchair. I have an awful feeling in the pit of my stomach.

"What have I done now?" I ask.

"I am going to make sure you become a proper young lady," Anne says.

Anne is pushing me down the hallway at a high speed.

"What have I done that is so bad?"

"The fact that you're still talking says everything."

"Everything about what? You are not making any sense," I say, trying to steady my voice.

"How you disrespect man's culture."

Anne stops abruptly, causing me to fling forward, hitting the ground of an unfamiliar room. I crawl and turn myself around to find my new friend chained to a wall.

"Emily!" I scream.

"How far are you willing to save your friend?" Anne asks in a devilish tone.

"You can't do this," Emily says desperately.

"Who is going to stop me?"

Emily and I don't say anything. She's right. No one is going to stop her. I look at Anne, who is searching through her pockets. She pulls out a gun and points it at Emily.

"Why do you need a gun in a place like this?" I ask.

"To keep order, and since there are no gun regulations, I can have as many as I want."

Damn, our fucking country.

"How far are you willing to go to save your friend?"

"I'll change."

"I don't believe you. You won't change on your own."

I hear a loud popping sound, a sound I've heard enough times to recognize. I look over at Emily. The bullet tore into her chest.

"What are you going to do to help her, nothing?"

I try to crawl over to Emily through my pain, but Anne blocks my way.

"Let this be a reminder to you. Think about this the next time you want to rebel."

I feel a sharp pinch in my neck and fall into darkness.

Chapter Eight

I wake up a few days later with a light in my eyes and an IV in my arm. I move my feet; they no longer hurting. What the hell did they give me that I healed this fast? The curtain next to me opens up.

"Oh good. You're awake," Hans says.

"How long have I been out?" I ask.

"We will discuss that later, but we have to go now."

"Where are we going?"

Hans leads me over to the window, where I see a rope hanging.

"Climb down."

I crawl out the window and down the rope carefully. Hans does the same.

"Follow me to the car—quickly!"

I advance with Hans to the van. He drives off.

"How much time-"

"Shh, the van has a camera."

I sit in silence for half an hour until Hans suddenly stops the van; he touches me on the shoulder.

"Follow me."

I follow Hans to an average-looking black car, and we drive for another hour and a half. We come to an eerie-looking mountain covered in fog. After a short drive, we reach the top to find a cozy log cabin. It looks fairly modern with some rustic touches. The log cabin has a quaint living room, a kitchen, and a small dining room.

"Welcome to my home," Hans says.

"Thank you," I say.

"Honey, can you please come downstairs. We have a guest."

I watch a woman descend the stairs. She needs no introduction.

"Hello Niema," Malene says.

"Malene? Can someone tell me what the hell is going on?

"Please sit down," Malene says.

I sit down in a rocking chair while Hans and Malene sit down on a couch.

"Malene works in the jail where the Moral's Police bring their victims. She saw you, and right away she knew you were going to be sent to Anne's facility. She called me, and we began to make a plan to get you out."

"How could you have known that?"

"Anne made a deal with Judge Pitts. Anne gets paid for every girl sent to the facility, and a percentage of that payment goes to him."

"How long has that deal been going on?"

"Ten years."

"How long have I been out?"

"You've been in a medically induced coma for four months."

"I don't understand. Why would Anne want that?"

"If you are seen as a troubled girl, they try to get you addicted to drugs so you are more submissive and less likely to cause trouble."

"Am I addicted to heroin or some other illegal drug now?"

"No, that is why I got you out when I did."

A moment of silence fills the room.

"Is Emily dead?"

"Yes, I'm so sorry."

"How did Anne get away with that?"

"The guards cleaned up the blood, and they put Emily's body in the surrounding woods. They said she tried to escape and became violent when they were attempting to capture her."

"Does her family know that she is gone?" I ask.

"Yes, and they don't care," Hans says.

"Well, she did break the rules. Why did the two of you want to rescue me?

"We want to get you out of the United States," Malene says.

"Why?" I ask shocked.

"Someone has to tell the rest the world what is going on, and we believe that person is you."

"I don't think I am the right person for that. I mean how would I get out of the United States? Where would I go? What will become of my family?"

"We can talk about this in the morning; you need rest."

Hans goes to the kitchen, and Malene gets up from the couch.

"Follow me, dear."

I follow Malene upstairs. The upstairs is a tiny space with two bedrooms, a small hallway closet, and a bathroom. I follow Malene into the smaller of the two bedrooms. It is a modest, but cozy bedroom with a twin-sized bed, a nightstand, and a dresser.

"This was my daughter's room."

"Did she go back home?"

"No. She was a doctor at an abortion clinic. She was killed during the Baby Killer Riots."

"I'm sorry."

"That's alright; it happened a long time ago."

We fall into silence.

"I grew up near where the riots happened."

"Did you believe the lie? That the doctors were terrible people murdering babies."

"At first yes, but then I began to think for myself."

"You are quite the little fireball."

"I never tried to be."

"Get some sleep. We'll talk in the morning."

"What I am going to wear?"

Malene points to the closet.

"You and my daughter are of similar size. The clothes should fit you."

Malene leaves, and I rest on the bed. I think for a while, and I know what I have to do.

Chapter Nine

I wake up to the sound and smell of food cooking. I would think since I've been in a medically induced coma for four months I wouldn't be so tired. I head downstairs.

"Good morning," Hans says.

"Hello," I reply.

"How do you feel?"

"Tired."

"That's because the drugs are leaving your system. It will take a few days for the drugs to wear off."

"Have you thought about what you would like to do?" Malene asks.

"I want to leave, but I need to know the plan."

"We will use our car to get you across the border into Canada. And when we get there, you will fly to a country of your choosing."

"How is that going to work? By now, Anne has sent my picture to every law enforcement agency. What if I get caught?"

"We can change your appearance."

"But where will I go?"

"Anywhere you want."

"I've never thought about where I would go before."

"Have either of you ever been to England?"

"Yes, it's a beautiful place, Germany is a great place to live too," Hans says with a smile on his face.

"What if I change my mind? Can I leave?"

"Yes, travel restrictions are a little more lax. All you need is a passport."

"How am I going to get one of those?"

"We already have one for you."

Hans hands me a passport, and it looks close enough to the real thing.

"All we need is a name you can remember."

"What's a name that I can remember?" I say thinking aloud.

"Try to think of a common one," Malene says.

I think for a moment.

"Elizabeth Moore."

"Okay," Hans says.

"When are we leaving?"

"In a few days, when the drugs wear off," Hans says.

Hans puts pancakes on a plate.

"Do you eat pork?" Hans asks.

"No."

Hans hands me butter, and syrup, and I put them on my pancakes.

"How am I getting to England?"

"We have a friend with a plane. She will take you there," Malene says.

"What do I do once I get there?"

"Apply for asylum and tell the world what is going on here," Hans says.

"We both know what will happen to my mom and grandma if I talk."

"Niema, if you don't speak out, things will continue to go on the way they are," Malene says.

"I know," I say, ashamed.

I finish eating my breakfast, and I go upstairs to shower.

I am not brave; I am a coward. I am good at running away, but not at standing my ground. I can't fight the United States alone; I am only one person. I leave the shower and put on fresh clothes.

"I bet you haven't worn pants for a long time," Malene says.

"No, I haven't," I say, rubbing them.

"I know this is a lot to take in all at once."

"You have no idea."

"Niema, you have to be brave."

"I'm trying, but I have my mom and grandma to think about."

"I know it is hard to be brave. Could you live with yourself if you have the power to change people's suffering, and you do nothing to stop it?"

"You know what happens to people who defy the government."

"Millions of people are suffering right now."

I put my head down.

"I know."

"And you have to decide if you want to continue to let that happen or if you want to help stop it."

Malene walks away, and I realize that I have to make the most important choice of my life...

* * *

Three days later, I feel like myself again.

"It's time," Hans says.

"Are you sure?" I ask.

"The longer we stay here, the easier it is for someone to find you," Malene says.

"I don't have anything packed."

Hans hands me a bag.

"I took care of it for you," he says smiling.

I take the bag, and I follow Hans and Malene to the black car.

"How did this get here?"

"It's the car we took the day I broke you out of Anne's facility."

"I must have been out of it that day."

I get into the car. We dyed my hair last night, and now it's black. It looks natural enough, and we also cut it. I like it. It's one of the first times I've made a choice about my appearance. I am wearing a dress, but only until we get across the border.

"What are the two of you going to do?" I ask.

"We are heading back to Germany," Malene says.

"How long does it take to get to the border?"

"It will take us about an hour to get there," Hans says.

"What if they recognize me?"

"Stay calm and act like you are doing nothing wrong," Malene says.

"It's a good thing I haven't committed a crime," I say sarcastically. "Do you have family in Germany?"

"Yes, family and friends," Malene says.

"Where did you live in Germany?"

"Munich," Malene replies.

"Where did you grow up?" Hans asks.

"L.A, the same place where the Baby Killer Riots took place."

"How does the neighborhood look now?"

"The same as it did in 2016."

"Ah, so nothing ever really changes."

"No, it doesn't."

We reach the border, and I begin to feel a little queasy. I see miles of virgin wilderness, something I did not see a lot growing up in L.A.

"Why do you wish to cross the border?" an officer asks.

"My wife, daughter and I would like to see Canada," Hans says.

"Why? The United States is an incredible place."

"We have friends in Canada."

"I need to see your passports."

I hand mine to the front.

"Girl, why are you not from Germany?

"My parents were unreliable. These people took me in and raised me as a wholesome Christian girl."

"You look like that Levy girl."

"Well, I can assure you that I am not," I say in the dumbest tone possible.

"Who is the current president?"

"I'm a woman. I don't need to keep up with politics."

"Okay, you do not sound smart enough to be her."

He hands us back our passports, and we drive across the border. About twenty minutes later, we reach the closed gates of a private airport.

"Is the airport closed?" I ask.

"Not for us, it isn't," Hans says.

"Rosa, it's me. Hans," he speaks into an intercom.

I hear a noise, and the gates begin to open. We drive in, and I know I am no longer being held back: I can be a strong, confident woman in public. I am soaring.

Epilogue

It has been twenty years since I left the United States and settled in England. I have not missed the constant fear of being taken away or the oppression, but people no longer have to fear that. A little while after I left, I wrote an autobiography about my life in the United States; the world was shocked.

Around the globe and one by one, countries responded strongly, even better than I could have imagined. They cut ties with America. The economy collapsed, and the citizens revolted against their government. The first United States government and its laws were restored. We are right back to where we started. It took money to change the world; it's all about the money.

www.ingramcontent.com/pod-product-compliance
Lightning Source LLC
Chambersburg PA
CBHW071223130626
46555CB00004B/1817